Bob and Flo

Rebecca Ashdown

Houghton Mifflin Harcourt

Boston   New York

It was Flo's first day of preschool.

She had her lunch and a new bow.

"I like your bow," said a little penguin.
"I like your bucket," said another.
His name was Bob.

"Thanks," said Flo.

Flo tried some painting.

But then she noticed her bucket was missing,

and there was something different about . . .

Bob.

Flo went to look
for her bucket.

She found Bob playing with the blocks.

"I like your tower,"
said Flo.

"Thanks,"
said Bob.

Flo found some sand castles outside.

But where was her . . .

After lunch, Flo went to play on the slide.

There was her bucket!

But where was Bob?

Bob was stuck!

Flo knew what to do.

WHOOSH

went the water.

"Thanks!"
said Bob.

Then Bob and Flo went

WHOOSH

WHOOSH

until it was time to go home.

"Bye-bye, Flo!"
said Bob.

"See you tomorrow, Bob!" said Flo.
"And don't forget our bucket!"

For Tate and Rufus

Text and illustrations copyright © Rebecca Ashdown 2014
First published in the UK by Oxford University Press in 2014 as *Bob and Flo: The Missing Bucket*
First published in the United States in 2015 by Houghton Mifflin Harcourt

www.hmhco.com

The text type was set in Triplex Light.
The display type was set in Fredericka the Great.

Library of Congress Cataloging-in-Publication Data is available.
ISBN 978-0-544-44430-0

Manufactured in China
10 9 8 7 6 5 4 3 2 1
4500492219